My Best Friend

Written by Diane Namm
Illustrated by Mike Gordon

My First
READER

children's press ®

A Division of Scholastic Inc.
New York Toronto London Auckland Sydney
Mexico City New Delhi Hong Kong
Danbury, Connecticut

Library of Congress Cataloging-in-Publication Data

Namm, Diane.
  My best friend / written by Diane Namm ; illustrated by Mike Gordon.
      p. cm. – (My first reader)
Summary: A group of young boys and girls who each like different things, from playing with dolls
to riding go-carts to playing with puppies and kittens, finally find common ground and become friends.
  ISBN 0-516-24416-7 (lib. bdg.)   0-516-25504-5 (pbk.)
  [1. Best friends–Fiction. 2. Friendship–Fiction. 3.
Individuality–Fiction. 4. Stories in rhyme.] I. Gordon, Mike, ill. II.
Title. III. Series.
  PZ8.3.N27My 2004
  [E]–dc22
                                                  2003014071

OCT 7 2004

Note to Parents and Teachers

Once a reader can recognize and identify the 49 words used to tell this story, he or she will be able to successfully read the entire book. These 49 words are repeated throughout the story, so that young readers will be able to recognize the words easily and understand their meaning.

The 49 words used in this book are:

a	could	hat	my	towers
all	doll	have	new	we
always	flowers	heart	of	wear
and	forever	I	pet	were
baseball	friend	if	play	will
be	friends	in	puppy	with
best	gather	into	ride	would
candy	go-cart	let	sand	yes
car	gold	lots	share	you
cat	guppy	make	star	

Will you be my best friend,
always and forever?

If you were my best friend,
you could play with my new doll.

If you were my best friend, we could play with my baseball.

If you were my best friend,
you could play with my new puppy.

If you were my best friend,
I would let you have a guppy.

If you were my best friend, we could make sand into towers.

If you were my best friend,
we could gather lots of flowers.

If you were my best friend,
I would let you wear my hat.

If you were my best friend,
I would let you pet my cat.

21

If you were my best friend,
you could play with my best car.

If you were my best friend,
you could wear my new gold star.

If you were my best friend,
you could ride in my go-cart.

If we were all best friends,
we could share my candy heart.

Yes, we will be best friends,
always and forever.

ABOUT THE AUTHOR

Diane Namm is the author of more than twenty-five books for children and young adults. Formerly an editor in New York, Namm freelances for a children's entertainment production company, writes, and lives in Malibu, California, with her husband and two children. About *My Best Friend,* she wrote, "Best friends are hard to find, but I've been lucky enough to know a few. Some live nearby and others live far away, but in our hearts, we're together, just like the friends in this book."

ABOUT THE ILLUSTRATOR

Mike Gordon was born in England. He attended Rochdale College of Art, but followed the advice of his parents and became an engineer. At least until 1983, when he switched his career to freelance illustrator. Since then he has illustrated many children's books, and his work has been published in more than eighteen countries. Gordon has four children and has lived in California since 1993.

10-04

ER   Namm, Diane
        My best friend.

GAYLORD RG